AUTHOR: D.H. Parish
COVER ART: Kylee Thompson
FOUNDING EDITOR: Kevin Kortum

Table of Contents

I found the first body my second month on the force. I was assigned to the 15th—the Hawthorn Manor section of the city. There's a lot of development there nowadays: new condos sprouting up, old Victorians with "good bones" being gutted and remodeled for millionaires, and all sorts of chichi restaurants. Back then, Hawthorn was a pretty rough neighborhood, with as many homes abandoned as occupied, where it would have been easier to buy an eighth than a piece of sushi.

That night around eleven, I was driving alone in my squad car on Parkview waiting for the next call when my lights caught someone lying in the overgrown grass of Golden Park. Calling Golden Park a "park" is overly generous; it's a tiny lot near the corner of Parkview and 43rd—the former lawn of the dilapidated mansion next to it. It had earned the park designation only when the city seized the land to pay off back taxes. Anyway, I pulled over to make sure the person was okay, figuring I would find some druggie sleeping off his latest hit. I radioed in the stop and stepped out of my Crown Vic. Flashlight in hand, I walked toward the body. Because of the overgrowth, it wasn't until I was about 10 feet away when I realized he was a she and that, as her pale skin reflected the flashlight beam, she was completely naked—not a stitch of clothing in sight. She lay flat on her back, arms at her side, knees bent. Her head was turned away so I couldn't see her face. I announced myself and asked if she was okay. She didn't answer. I walked around her to get a look at her face, but a mess of disheveled black hair obscured it. I bent down and spoke again. No response. I pushed her hair away. Her eyes were wide open, which gave me a shock, and I jumped back up. She didn't move. She didn't even blink.

"Are you okay?" I asked again, louder.

Nothing.

My heart was beating a mile a minute. Although it was summer, it was cold enough that night to see my breath steaming upward, but I didn't see any coming from her. I bent down again and reached for her left wrist. Her skin felt warm, but there was no pulse. I called in what I'd found and started chest compressions. It took about five minutes for an ambulance and another squad car to arrive. It was a long five minutes. No one passed by while I rhythmically pounded on her rib cage, which gave out a crunch when I likely broke at least one of her ribs.

You don't forget your first body. She was probably in her late twenties, same as me. She was thin and short, with a round, pock-marked face and green eyes. Her black pupils were tightly constricted; her expression was of someone wincing against a bright light. It never changed the whole time I loomed over her, pressing again and again and again, one hundred times each minute in a desperate attempt to revive the dead. She had no track marks on her arms nor bruises on her limbs, only a poorly-healed surgical scar a bit south of her belly button.

The paramedics arrived just as I was tiring out. They pushed me out of the way and took over, but they confirmed after a few more minutes of futile CPR that she was gone. They loaded her on a stretcher, wheeled her into the back of their ambulance, and departed for the hospital morgue. Two other officers, both more experienced than I, showed up just after the paramedics. They took the lead, given how much of a rookie I was, and I wasn't about to object. We took photos and gathered what evidence we could, which was essentially nothing. Although the paramedics and I had trampled some of the tall grass, most of the lawn remained untouched, and we couldn't quite figure out how the woman had found her way into the middle of the park. If someone had carried and dumped her there, we couldn't find any footprints or tracks or signs of struggle. There was debris in the lot but nothing that might have been a weapon. We didn't find any fresh syringes or drug paraphernalia. And we never found her clothing.

The woman could not be identified. She didn't fit the profile in any missing person reports, and no one ever tried to claim the body. This was still the early days of DNA evidence, but everything we tried led nowhere. She had a smallpox vaccine scar on her left arm, so we thought she might have been an undocumented immigrant, perhaps explaining why no one was looking for her.

The postmortem didn't help much either. There was no evidence of rape or other sexual assault. Toxicology screens showed heroin in her system. That was a little odd; crack was the drug of choice in the 15th at that time, although we still found heroin occasionally. She was anemic, the coroner said, but not enough that it would have killed her, and again no good explanation for it. It could have been someone dumped her from somewhere else, but she was too warm to have been dead for long. At first I wondered if she weren't some rich white suburbanite who had traveled into the 15th for an adventure, hence the slightly unusual narcotic, but then someone would have been looking for her. Besides, the precinct was an equal opportunity mix of the downtrodden of many races, so she was more likely homegrown. In any event, she hadn't suffered respiratory failure, so the heroin didn't kill her.

The abdominal surgical scar turned out to have been from a hysterectomy; the coroner's report noted the procedure had been crudely done, but complications from it were not the cause of death. In fact, the coroner wasn't really sure why she died, except that all her systems had shut down, as if someone just flipped the off switch.

In short, the woman was a mystery. Homicide took over and investigated briefly; they gave up after two weeks. For them she was just a vagrant junkie, a lost soul not worth their time.

I didn't find the second body; Jack Wilson did. Jack, a ten-year veteran at the time, discovered her while on patrol *exactly* one month later. Same story: nighttime between eleven and midnight, naked white woman in her twenties, Golden Park, heroin in her system, dead but warm, no sexual assault. Again, she couldn't be identified. This revived the first case. Jack and I tried to follow any leads we could, questioned neighbors, leaned on informants, but no one seemed to have a clue about what was going on, or at least they weren't willing to tell us.

Although Jack went along with me on this investigation, he didn't care much about it. He told me he'd seen enough druggies die in the precinct in strange ways to know this was likely just another pathetic lost life. Unless I could find some new angle, it wasn't worth our time. No doubt, part of his disinterest was that he'd been promoted to sergeant and was awaiting transfer to a different precinct, one where you weren't, in his words, "just cleaning up society's trash."

I did care. I got authorization to set up surveillance cameras at Golden Park. The technology wasn't as good then, and the CCTV system often failed, but I hoped it might provide evidence if something else happened—maybe we could save someone. I would regularly pass by Golden Park at least a few times every shift. Like Jack, most of the old timers thought I was wasting my time. Even those who gave me encouragement did so primarily because they thought it would knock the naiveté out of me and get me to focus on more important cases.

They were wrong.

My work paid off one month later. As I cruised by Golden Park around 11:30 on a Tuesday night, I saw rustling in the thin tall grass, now turned to hay. I pulled over, radioed for backup, and dashed toward the motion. I found a white man, his pants pulled down below his knees, bent over a naked white woman. The guy had one hand on her neck, the other on her hip. I ordered him to stop, but he ignored me. I grabbed his shoulders and yanked him off, hurling him to his back on the ground beside her. I drew my service revolver–the first time I ever did that in the line of duty–and held it a few feet from his face. He looked up at me, his expression dazed and confused. I yelled at him to roll over onto his belly and put his arms at his side. He didn't move, so I kicked him a few times. He finally got the idea and complied. I cuffed him behind his back and searched his pockets; he had a baggie of weed and a switchblade, which I tossed to the side.

I then attended to the woman, who hadn't moved this whole time. No pulse. No breath. She was already dead.

I looked back at the man, pointing my flashlight at him. He presented a pathetic picture with his cuffed hands lying over his pale, acne-riddled, exposed ass. He looked up at me with a dumb, glazed expression. "Hey man, what's goin' on?" he asked.

"What's goin' on," I said, "is that you're under arrest for rape and murder."

"What the hell, man," he replied through his scraggly beard, "I didn't do shit." I read him his rights, but he kept talking. "I was just minding my own business, and that chick appeared outta nowhere."

"She appeared out of nowhere?" I asked.

"Yeah. Like, she wasn't there, then she was. I was just takin' care of my own business when I saw her. I was just checkin' on her."

"Checking on her? With your pants down?"

"Hey man, I told you, I was takin' care of my own business. You never done that? I didn't fuck her. I didn't even have the chance."

"So you're saying you would have if you'd had the chance?"

"Look man, if she let me, sure. But I ain't no rapist."

"You been here before?"

"In Golden? Yeah, of course. I live around here. I pass by all the time. Is that a crime now too? I didn't fuck her."

"So you just strangled her?"

"What? I didn't strangle her."

"So how did you kill her?" I paused, but he didn't answer. "You know we've got cameras here. We'll be able to see everything your sorry ass did. And it does look quite sorry."

He stayed quiet, just looking at me, so I continued. "She isn't the first woman you killed here, is she? It might go easier on you if you'd just tell me what you did with her and the others. I can put in a good word with the DA. I promise you, I'll be a lot nicer than the backup that's on its way. Without cooperation, you're looking at a date with the executioner."

He stuttered a reply, "I... I... I didn't even have the chance to do anything. Oh man, cameras? I think I better talk to a lawyer."

"That's your right."

He was silent for about a minute. I bagged the weed and switchblade. "Just so you know, we're also going to bring you in for possession."

"Oh fuck." He stopped straining looking at me from his awkward position and slumped to the ground.

That was the last time we ever spoke. The third woman fit the pattern of the first two. Like them, she was never identified. The only unusual fact about her was that she had tuberculosis, which supported the theory that the guy was preying on immigrants.

The cameras I'd set up were, true to form, glitchy. They showed nothing happening about 15 minutes prior to my arrival, then went to static until they turned on again when they caught the perp, who had the misfortunate name of Lester Jackson Shaggrass, in his wrestling position over the woman. Lester was leaning over her for about twenty seconds, his penis visibly erect, before you could see me throwing him off her. The lab found his semen on her; the defense lawyer argued at trial that it could have simply dripped on her because Lester had been masturbating before he found her, but even if the jury had bought that theory, it didn't win him any points. Hell, the papers started calling the guy "Jack the Dripper."

The exact cause of death remained a bit of a mystery, but the time of death was confirmed to be within the hour I found her. We couldn't find enough evidence to charge Lester with the other two murders, but the judge let the prosecutors introduce them as part of his pattern. Lester never testified. He had a history of indecent exposure, low level robberies, and drug convictions that, had they come up at trial, would not have endeared him to the jury.

I, on the other hand, proved to be the star witness whose diligence and police work helped stop this budding serial killer. Turned out I was a natural in the courtroom, and my testimony plus the evidence I found was enough to get Lester convicted of rape and felony murder. My picture in the paper also got me quite a few dates. More importantly, in the nine months between Lester's arrest and trial, no other women were found. The killings stopped. He was the one.

Lester was sentenced to death. The appeals process took five years to run its course, which was actually pretty fast. The execution took place at the state facility near the capital, and I was present to watch him die from the lethal cocktail. No one ever missed him.

Breaking the Golden Park case made my career. I received a special citation from the city, and the precinct captain, Lane Clinton, took me under his wing. I was put on the fast track for promotion, making captain in only my twelfth year. Capt. Clinton took retirement when I reached that milestone on the condition I would succeed him. Under my leadership, the 15th became a model precinct. Everyone expected I would become the next commissioner; a few political operatives and one newspaper editorial even suggested I skip that post and run for mayor.

IV

Almost twenty-five years to the day after the first woman was found, I was woken around 1:00 AM when dispatch put through a call from an officer in her first week on the job.. She was calling from University Hospital, she said, nervously explaining that a young woman had been brought into the ER after a passerby who was taking his dog for a nighttime walk found her lying naked and unconscious in Golden Park. So far there was no evidence of rape or other signs of violence. The nurse caring for the patient was old enough to remember the original series of Golden Park murders and called the police. The woman was stable but still unconscious. The officer apologized profusely for not waiting until the morning to call me, but she had thought that I would want to know about the situation sooner given my history. I reassured her that she had done the right thing and that I would get over there shortly.

I dressed quickly and drove the twenty minutes to the hospital. I flashed my badge to the triage nurse, who let me through the ER's locked doors, and found the woman in a back holding room for patients awaiting beds on the floors. The officer who called me was standing outside her room, which was separated from the ER's chaos only by thin blue drapes. The rookie cop, her voice quivering, introduced herself as Officer Santiago and explained she had arrived only about ten minutes before telephoning me. She hadn't gone in to see the victim yet, but while she'd been waiting, the woman had moaned a few times without saying anything coherent. Santiago also introduced me to the nurse who called her. I thanked Santiago for her work, reassuring her she'd done the correct thing by contacting me and that she should never be afraid to do what she thought was right. I dismissed her back to her beat and she seemed visibly relieved she hadn't blown it.

The nurse, who spoke to me as he sat typing at his workstation, said he remembered the original case (he confessed it had stuck with him because he'd seen my picture in the paper and thought I was cute). The patient was a short white woman, likely in her twenties, although they couldn't say more because she had no ID on her. Her vitals had been stable since she'd arrived. She had some heroin in her system, but toxicology was otherwise clear. Her hemoglobin was low, but her labs were otherwise normal. A head CT was negative; the doctor was considering a full body scan to look for bleeding given the anemia, although the count was not low enough to warrant a transfusion. The doctor wasn't quite sure why she wasn't fully awake yet, so they admitted her for monitoring and a neurology consult.

The patient had spoken a few times, but never said anything anyone could understand or that might have been useful to figure out what happened to her. Because of her cognitive issues, they'd strapped her to the bed to prevent any falls.

I thanked the nurse and pushed past the curtain into what passed for the patient's room. She was lying in a hospital gown, an IV hooked into her left arm, several white canvas bands over her body at intervals securing her to the bed. Multiple leads came off of her chest, which visibly rose with each breath. A monitor behind her periodically beeped for reasons I didn't understand.

I pulled up a chair next to her and sat down to wait for her to wake up. As I studied her, I realized she looked quite similar to the very first woman I'd found all those years ago. When she opened her green eyes a few minutes later, my heart leapt into my throat: she looked almost identical.

"Where... where am I?" she asked, her voice dry and cracking.

"You're in University Hospital, ma'am. You were found unconscious in Golden Park."

"Did it..? Did I..? Where is..?" She said as she turned her head side-to-side to look around the room.

"Ma'am, I'm Captain Raymond. Can you tell me your name?"

Her eyes suddenly went wide. "We need to find pea! We need to find pea!" She started moving her shoulders, struggling against the restraints.

"What is pea?" I asked

"Ay, we need to find pea, save pea." Her voice became less hoarse as she talked, beginning to betray some accent, possibly Russian.

"We'll find pea, I promise. But please, tell me who you are." I leaned in closer as I spoke

"He will get pea." She said.

"Is pea a person? Is pea a woman?"

"He will get pea next." She said louder, becoming more frantic.

I tried responding as calmly as I could. "Who is he? Do you remember what he looks like?"

She paused before answering, raising her head as much as the restraints allowed. "He will toot!" she yelled. "He will toot!" The monitor started beeping rapidly.

I stood up and leaned over her, putting my hands on her arms to try and soothe her. "It's okay." I whispered. "Try to stay calm. I'm a police officer. I'm here to help. Speak slowly so I can understand." She looked at me with those green eyes, now filled with tears. She went still for a few seconds and then started thrashing and yelling. I felt a tap on my shoulder.

"What in God's name are you doing to my patient?" a voice behind me said with a slight German accent. I turned to see a man clad in blue scrubs and a long white doctor's coat. He had short-cropped black hair and wire-rim glasses. "She needs rest. Please leave her alone!"

"I'm Captain Raymond. This woman may have been the victim of ..."

"That does not concern me," he cut me off, as she continued to strain against the straps holding her down, shouting something like "her table! her table!" "This woman is clearly in distress, and you are jeopardizing her health. Please leave at once." I followed his order. As I passed through the blue curtains to exit the room, I saw him extract a syringe from his jacket pocket. Within seconds, the woman had calmed down; he must have given her something strong.

"There," the doctor said, emerging from the room. "She needs rest. In the morning may you speak with her. She will not go anywhere. Please, kindly leave."

I was not used to being told what to do, but I supposed he was right, and I didn't want to cause a scene. I was never one for abusing the privileges of my office. I left and went home to go back to bed.

V

I didn't sleep well that night and returned to the hospital at 8:00 AM. It took me a while to find where they moved her. Unfortunately, I learned, it was to the morgue. She died about an hour after I left. Her body just shut down— shock, they said. Still no identification. I got some blood and DNA samples for our labs and left for the precinct. I found Officer Santiago at a desk processing paperwork. I pulled her aside and told her not to write anything up about the woman from yesterday and to give me whatever she had—I would take care of it.

I walked into my office, closed the door, and slunk into the black leather chair behind my desk. What the hell was going on? The most likely explanation was some kind of copycat. But, why now, twenty-five years later? If it was a copycat, to what end? Another, far more distressing thought, nagged at me: maybe it was the same perp, coming back for more after all these years. Maybe I had never solved the case.

I gripped the specimen bag of samples I had taken from the hospital in my pocket and held them up in front of me. DNA evidence would be better now, so maybe we could get better leads. But that would require explaining what I was looking for. Before opening that can of worms, I thought I ought to take a look at the scene first. I put the bag in my top desk drawer and locked it in safely. Then I left the station and drove to Golden Park.

I hadn't paid any attention to Golden in a while. It was still not much of a park, although the grass was trimmed, and its whole presentation was much nicer in keeping with the revived neighborhood. A construction fence sealed off the adjacent old mansion; someone finally purchased it and was remodeling. The park itself was empty save for a woman walking a Bichon Frise, and they ignored me. I walked systematically through the park, back and forth as if mowing a lawn, to ensure I covered every inch of it, scouring the place for any evidence of what might have happened the night before. I found nothing.

I drove back to the station, wondering what to do. Most likely, I concluded, this was just a weird coincidence. Like President Lincoln having a secretary named Kennedy and President Kennedy having a secretary named Lincoln. If so, that was the end. If the new girl were the victim of a copycat, there wasn't much evidence to go on, and as unfortunate as it was, we'd need to wait for him to strike again. If it was the first killer back at it, as unlikely as that was, we were in the same predicament.

What shouldn't happen, I knew, was to let any of this become public. Doing that would only let whoever was out there know we were watching. And, if this got out, no matter what the reality, the *real* next victim would be me. I would never become commissioner, not to mention mayor. Even if I had made some kind of mistake, I'd done great things over the past twenty-five years. I was a good cop. It would be wrong to let one small error from long ago wipe away all I had done and *would still do* for this city. Moreover, even if Lester hadn't been the one to kill that girl, he was definitely about to rape her. The world was better without scum like him.

So I would watch and wait. There would be no formal investigation yet. Rather, I would see how things played out. I let the specimens sit in my desk for now.

For the next month, nothing happened. One Friday morning, Commissioner Kelly's secretary called me and told me Kelly wanted to see me in his office at headquarters that afternoon. She didn't say why. When I got there, the secretary escorted me in and quickly left, closing the door behind her. The commissioner, a large man with a large voice, remained seated behind his vast mahogany desk.

"Andy," he said, motioning with his hands, "have a seat." He had a poker face, and I had no idea what was coming. He sensed my apprehension and let me stew in it.

"Andy, I had you come here today to let you know," he paused a bit before breaking out into a wide grin, "I'm planning to announce my retirement next week and the mayor is going to appoint you to replace me. Congratulations."

My shoulders untensed, and I breathed a sigh of relief.

"I think," Kelly continued, "the mayor was worried you might run against her. Hold your friends close and your enemies closer, they say. Anyway, you'll do a great job." He stood up and put out his right hand.

"Thank you, sir," I replied, moving forward to shake it. "It will be hard to follow you."

"Yes, it will. And now for your first lesson in politics. The mayor has a request: a man named Douglas Jessups wants to meet you. He's a rich donor to her campaign; he also writes checks to the Police Benevolent Foundation. I told her I'd give you the details. When you take the job, you'll have to start doing a lot of this sort of thing. Nothing compromising, of course. No one is above the law. The rich just want to feel they have access, be able to say they know people. You can decline, but if you plan on going further, you'll want to say yes."

"I'm happy to meet Mr. Jessups," I said with enthusiasm.

"Of course you are," he said as he pulled a business card out of his pocket and handed it to me. "Details are on it. I think he wanted to meet you at eight."

"Tonight?" I asked, pocketing the card without looking at it.

"Yes, tonight. Which," he said, walking over to a corner cabinet, "still gives us time for some celebratory scotch."

He poured us each a glass and raised a toast to my future. I thanked him for all his support.

"My support? That didn't mean anything. You've been in line for the job since the day you got Jack the Dripper. Anyway, don't tell anyone about this until the formal announcement at the press conference. It'll be at the mayor's office a week from today at 3:00 PM. Wear your dress blues."

I left the commissioner's office walking on air. I stopped by my office on the way home to get my case. Couldn't help but hum the old "Jeffersons" theme song to myself as I passed through the 15th. Before I could leave, however, Officer Santiago knocked on my door.

"Sorry to bother you, Captain, but can I speak to you briefly?" she asked.

"Of course," I said.

She walked in and closed the door behind her. "I wanted to let you know that I had surveillance cameras placed around Golden Park, and... "

"Why did you do that?" I asked. "I specifically told you not to investigate. You directly disobeyed me."

"I'm sorry, I... I... I couldn't stop thinking about that woman. I knew Golden Park was where you made your reputation pursuing a case that seemed hopeless, so I thought it might help, and,"

"Who authorized this?" I demanded.

"No one, sir. I did it on my own," she said.

"Who else knows about this?" I asked.

"No one, sir," she said.

I paused for a few seconds. "Well?" I asked.

"Well what? sir," she said.

"What've you found?"

"Nothing yet, sir," she said.

I looked at my watch, then back at the rookie, who was now visibly shaking. "Officer Santiago, what you did was a gross violation of your authority and your duty. Do you understand that you can be fired for this?"

"I... I... I..."

"Santiago, you are not on this case. There is no case for you to be on. Anything you have or have recorded should be given to me in hard copy and all other traces destroyed. Any monitoring you are doing is now over."

"Yes sir," she stuttered.

"I am, for the moment, going to let this slide, but consider yourself on probation. If you step out of line in any way over the next three months, you will be turning in your badge. If you ever pursue another case like this on your own initiative, you are done. Do we understand each other?"

Santiago nodded. I was about to order her to take down the surveillance cameras immediately but then thought better of it. Santiago personally set up the cameras so her fingerprints would be on them. If any problems arose about conducting unauthorized surveillance, it would all fall back on her. I could use the cameras and anything they captured without anyone else knowing. So I opted not to say anything about them.

"That is all. Leave," I said.

Santiago, head down, backed out of my office and slowly closed the door behind her.

VI

Needing a break from the whirlwind of events that afternoon, I went home to get ready for my evening meeting. As I took off my pants to shower, I fished the card from the pocket to look at the address. 4266 Parkview Avenue. It took a second for me to register that it was the mansion at Golden Park! What the hell? Was this some kind of a joke? Was Kelly or someone else on to my secret? Did this "donor" know something about the Golden Park killer? If this was a coincidence, it was a hell of a coincidence. I made up my mind to carry a weapon with me on the visit.

I arrived at 8:00 PM sharp, parking a block away. A tall man in a well-tailored blue suit and a white shirt, collar unbuttoned, stood at the entrance to the construction fence. He stepped toward me as I approached.

"Captain Raymond, so nice to meet you," he said, extending his hand.

"Mr. Jessup?" I asked, extending my own to accept his greeting.

"Yes, but please, call me Douglas. Let's go inside, shall we?"

He swung open the fence gate, and I followed him in. "The neighborhood's much nicer than it once was, but we still need to be careful until the construction's done," he explained as he locked the gate behind us with a metal chain and padlock. I discreetly pressed my left arm against my breast to feel the reassuring firmness of my holstered gun. We walked up to the front entrance, Jessups leading the way, along a path that was still just packed dirt. The front doorway appeared to be a restored antique, a weighty and imposing dark oak bulwark. "Had this brought in from Europe, from the rectory of an old Gothic church," he explained proudly as we passed through it.

He led me into a large walnut-paneled living room lit by standing lamps. There were two dark brown leather chairs in front of a massive stone fireplace with a small table in between. He offered me a seat in one while he took the other.

"Captain, I'm a man of business, so let's get to it. I bought this mansion about a year ago. The place needed to be gutted and remodeled, most of which is done. Looking at the deed, my attorney realized that in the transaction, Golden Park and its land would also revert back to me. The city was going to fight it, but I agreed to continue to allow public use of the park for the next few years before I made it private again. On the merits of my position, they agreed to my terms. That and a contribution to the mayor's reelection campaign, of course."

"My architect said it would be easy for us to extend the basement into the land under Golden Park. I wanted a screening room, and this would be the place for it. Well, when we started digging, about 10 feet in, we began finding these." He reached into his pocket, pulled out a white cloth that had been folded over several times, and handed it to me.

I unwrapped it. Inside was a piece of bone.

"I believe it's a metacarpal," he said. "Human."

"When did you find this?"

"Earlier this week. That's why I wanted you to come."

"To open a murder investigation?"

"Ah, no. I don't think that's going to be, ah, the right thing."

"What do you mean?"

"It'll be easier if I show you. Follow me."

He led me to stairs that descended into a vast basement. Construction lights hung on strings along the perimeter, giving the appearance we were walking into a cave network. We stopped in front of what looked like a part of the wall, but when he pushed on one part of it, it opened to reveal a tunnel behind the wall with wooden beams supporting the structure. The tunnel itself did not have lighting so Jessup took out his phone and turned on its flashlight, illuminating the darkness. He motioned me to walk forward. I stepped in about 4 feet.

"Dear God!" I gasped when I realized what I was looking at. There were numerous skeletons, intertwined in grotesque arrays, bones poking out from where the digging had stopped like some horrific bas relief.

"I counted at least 40 distinct skulls before I stopped," Jessup said matter-of-factly. "No clothing, no jewelry, no other artifacts. Just bones. Lots and lots of bones.

"We're gonna have to open an investigation here," I said, still staring at the ghastly menagerie.

"Are you?" he asked. "I don't think that will be necessary."

I tensed my right arm, moving it slowly toward the gun at my chest, readying to draw, but for the moment keeping my back to Jessup so he couldn't see what I was doing. "Why don't you think it will be necessary?" I replied.

"Because," he said, "at best it's a very cold case. Those bodies must have been here for well over fifty years, if not longer."

"What do you mean?" I turned around to face him.

"Let's talk back upstairs away from this past grimness," he said. I followed him out of the basement, and we again, sat down in those leather chairs.

"The basement wall," he continued, "was intact when we started digging, so no one had been using the mansion while it was abandoned to hide bodies. You've been in the district for your whole career, right? You haven't seen anyone dig up Golden Park in the past twenty years, have you?"

He paused for a moment; I could see him trying to gauge my reaction. "Whatever happened here, happened long ago. There's no record of any cemetery here. Was this an Indian burial ground? Was some lunatic hiding his kills? Was some medical institution dumping bodies? Quite frankly, I don't care. It's all in the past. And in the past is where it needs to stay. What I don't want, what I won't tolerate, is any investigation. I plan to live in this mansion, and if this gets out, best case scenario is some fruitless inquiry that goes on for months or even years. Worst case, some group gets the government to forbid any construction on 'sacred land.'"

"So why are you telling me this?" I asked. "I'm the police. Investigating is what we do, what we have to do. Not to recommend breaking the law, but why'd you bring me here in the first place? Why didn't you just dump the bones?"

"Because," he continued, "I didn't want to risk them being found and getting caught. That would only make matters worse. No, I want your help getting rid of them."

I couldn't decide if Jessup was just an arrogant rich guy, a bit crazy, or both. "I'm sorry Douglas, but I can't. With what you've told me, even if it's a complete dead end, I have to open a case."

"Oh, I don't think you will," he said. "You see, I was understandably worried about theft and vandalism during the construction, so I had multiple security cameras set up. They picked up one of your officers placing her own cameras in Golden Park, which is to say, she invaded my private property. Did she have a warrant to do that?"

I didn't answer.

"I didn't think so. It wouldn't be a good look for the mayor to appoint a commissioner who conducts illegal surveillance on an innocent and upstanding citizen, would it? A citizen whose only crime is investing in his community and helping revive a once-blighted neighborhood?"

Jessup paused to let this sink in.

"So, Captain," he went on, "this is what's going to happen. You'll have the cameras in Golden Park removed in the next twelve hours. Then you're going to be here on Sunday morning at five to help supervise my crew move the bones to an incinerator, where you'll wait until they are reduced to unidentifiable ash. You will ensure no one interferes or asks questions, and that there is nothing to see. That's all. I'm not asking you to let a murderer go free. I just want to enjoy my home undisturbed by the past. Do we understand each other?"

I took a deep breath. Did I have a choice? I nodded slowly.

"I will take that as a yes. I believe our meeting is over. Good night, Captain Raymond. Thank you for coming." We stood up, and he escorted me outside, unlocking the fence to let me through. "Unless anything goes wrong," he said in parting, "I look forward to next Friday's announcement."

I drove home, grabbed a bottle of Jack, gave myself a healthy pour, and swallowed it in one gulp while standing at my kitchen counter. I refilled the glass and collapsed into a chair. I had agreed with Jessup to get out of there, but could I really do what he wanted—ignore dozens of dead bodies? That was wrong, against every reason I became a cop. But, as he pointed out, whoever those skeletons were, they all died many years ago. They're beyond help. Anyone who ever cared about what happened to them was long since dead. If Jessup knew about next Friday, he wasn't bluffing. I've done so much good as captain, and I would do so much more good as commissioner. Some small compromises are necessary along the way.

On the other hand, why not just come clean? So I don't get the commissioner job, was that so bad? Damn Santiago. Damn that woman in the hospital. Sure, she looked a little like the first body, but I only saw her for a minute. It was just my mind playing tricks on me. Heroin addicts all sorta blend together anyway. Should I throw it all away because of that? But then why didn't I have our lab process her blood? What was I worried about?

The liquor finally took enough of a hold to force me to sleep on my thoughts. If I had any dreams that night, I didn't remember them. When I woke, I knew what I would do. I called Santiago and told her she had one hour to remove and destroy every camera she'd placed in Golden Park. I then set an alarm for 4:30 AM the next day.

VII

It was dark and cold when I arrived outside the mansion early Sunday morning. A guy covered head to toe in a white hazmat suit leaving only his face visible stood by the fence waiting. "Here for the loading?" he asked, a slight but indeterminate accent in his voice. I nodded. He unlocked the gate and, after we walked in, chained it again behind us. There was a plain white truck, the size and shape of a U-Haul, parked in front of the mansion entrance, its sliding cargo door open, with several canvas bags lying next to it.

He jumped into the back. "Would you please help me with these bags?" I picked them up one by one and handed them to him. He threw them out of sight deep into the truck's hold, each one landing with a thud.

"Where's Jessup?" I asked as we walked inside. He told me Jessup had left after letting him in. He suggested I wait inside while he finished loading. I asked him how much longer it would take and he guessed another forty-five minutes or so. It would have gone faster, he said, except his partner, *the bastard*, was probably somewhere sleeping off a hangover and hadn't shown up.

I followed him to the basement and watched as he dug into the earth to wrench out the skeletons—plucking femurs, skulls, and ribs from the dirt and shoveling them into bags like they were fall leaves. Not wanting to see more, I climbed upstairs and roamed the mansion's first floor. After looking at the living room where Jessup and I talked, I wandered into the kitchen, which was gutted, ancient plumbing and wires exposed like the innards of a corpse in a forensics lab, while drop cloths covered the floors. I discovered in one corner a folding table set up with a laptop and two large monitors. The monitors showed live video from various cameras around the perimeter of the house. I pressed a key on the laptop, and the home screen for the surveillance system came up without requesting a password. I looked around to make sure the guy loading bones wouldn't be able to see me as he continued his work. Given the age of the mansion, the kitchen was designed to be hidden from the living areas so a family would never have to see their servants toiling. I figured out which camera was which and then searched for footage from the two that looked into Golden Park on the night last month when the most recent woman was discovered.

The video I found looked like something out of Star Trek. The park was empty and quiet, with no movement or activity, and then... the woman just materialized out of thin air naked, as if she'd been teleported. I double checked to make sure there wasn't some glitch in the film, but the time stamps were consistent. She lay there for about five minutes before the dog came into view sniffing her. I rewatched the video multiple times trying to decipher the trick. After the fourth or fifth time, I heard the worker call out. I quickly closed the search and returned the program to the home screen. I walked out of the kitchen through a back corridor and then into the living room and around toward the front entrance, where I saw him.

"What's up? Are you done?" I asked.

He turned around and said, "I finished the loading, but I found something behind the skeletons."

"What?" I asked.

"Perhaps you should take a look."

I followed him to the basement and back through the tunnel. The bones were cleared away, but behind where they had been was what looked like the side of a wooden crate.

"Should we try to open it?" he asked. "I am not looking for more work, but I would prefer not to be called to come back for this."

I looked at my watch. It was almost 6:00. I was about to say we should ignore it and just go to the incinerator so I could be done with this. Then I realized the small tunnel that had been created led out into Golden Park. From the looks of it, it was getting pretty close to just below the location where the women had been found each time.

"Sure," I said.

"I will need your help to dig, if you please," he said, handing me a shovel. He took up a pickaxe, and we cleared out what at first seemed to be the side of a large crate before revealing itself to be large enough to be an entire wall, almost eight feet high and ten feet wide, with thicker supporting beams on each side and in the middle. As I wondered what to do, my companion made the decision for us and started hacking into the thinner part of the wall, the wood easily splintering under his blows. It took only five hacks for him to open a hole large enough for us to walk through. The construction lights in the tunnel were not enough to shine past thehole so he went back out to retrieve flashlights and handed me one.

I walked through the jagged opening and wandered into an unexpectedly cavernous room. The air was stale, the odor of fresh earth from the excavation replaced by an antiseptic dryness. The space looked like an old laboratory, with the walls in front of me and to my left lined with wooden tables and shelves which held various glass beakers, tubes, and all the other equipment I dimly remembered from high school chemistry. In the center of the room sat what appeared to be an antique hospital gurney, still made up with white sheets. Everything was covered in a thin layer of dust.

Next to the wall on the right as we entered was what looked like a large black steamer trunk or one of those boxes magicians put their assistants in to saw them in half, except there were cables and wires coming out of one end. I knelt down next to it, placing one hand on the top, looking for a way to open whatever it was. "What is this?" I asked, not realizing I was talking out loud. At that moment something hard smashed into my skull. I heard a voice say, "You will find out," before everything went black.

VIII

When I came to, I was lying on my back, knees bent, head throbbing. I tried to rub the ache but couldn't as straps held my wrists and ankles tight. My vision was obstructed except for the sliver of a view above me, a view like the one you might have if thrown into the trunk of a car with the trunk lid left slightly ajar. The pungent smell of gasoline wafted into my tight space. As my eyes adjusted to the dim light, I could see I was still in the same underground room and, from what I could guess, inside the box I had been inspecting. I could hear some sort of tapping on the box near my feet and that guy muttering and occasionally yelling. I couldn't make out the words, although it sounded as if he were cursing in a foreign language.

I pulled against the restraints. The ankles and left wrist wouldn't budge, but the one on my right wrist started to give ever so slightly. Focusing on this, I rocked my right arm back and forth, back and forth, the strap biting into my skin but gaining slightly more slack with each motion until it ripped free, forcing my hand to jerk upward and nearly hit the lid above me.

I massaged my still aching head. My hair felt matted and damp, likely with blood. I slid my hand inside my shirt and felt the reassuring presence of my gun; he hadn't disarmed me when he knocked me out and tied me up. I reached over and struggled to undo the strap on my left wrist. I probably wouldn't be able to free my legs without disturbing the lid and alerting him. I would have to catch him off guard.

My arms now free, I took one deep breath and bolted upright, as if doing a sit up, pushing the lid up with my left hand and pointing my gun toward where I expected him to be.

Except he wasn't there. I scanned the room in the limited light of one flashlight laying where he should have been. No one. I placed the gun on my lap and worked at the straps on my feet. I got the left one off easily and was struggling to remove the right when I heard footsteps and saw the ray of another flashlight illuminate the hole before the man emerged through it, his hood now off.

"Stop!" I yelled. "Hands up!"

He froze and slowly raised his hands. He held a flashlight in one hand and a bundle of wire in the other. With my gun trained on him I worked my right foot free and stood up. A wave of nausea rolled over me as I rose. I had to fight to keep my balance.

I walked to the gurney in the middle of the room and picked up the other flashlight. "Get over in the corner over there and sit down" I said, motioning with the beam. He complied. I sat on the edge of the bed to rest.

"What the hell is going on?" I asked.

His lips curved into a smile. "Of course. Where should I begin?"

"Let's start with your name." I said.

"That is an unimportant question. You know, we have met before, Captain" he said, pausing to see if I recognized him. "In the hospital, when you were trying to speak with Goldie. Ah, Goldie. I did not want her to die, but she left me no choice," he said. "Maybe you do not recognize me without my glasses?"

I understood who Goldie must have been. "You were her doctor?" I asked.

"No, although I am a doctor. But it is easy to enter hospitals if you wear the right clothing and know how to act."

"You murdered her?"

"I loved her. But it was my only chance for success. After all I have done, I want to succeed. I need to succeed. I deserve to succeed. I will succeed."

"What do you mean?"

"This room you are in, this mansion you are in, this is my home. And that device you were in," he said, gesturing toward the box I had escaped, "is a time machine."

"A time machine?"

"Yes."

"You built a time machine?"

"No," he laughed. "I could never do that. I told you, I am a doctor. My brother Herman did. He was a genius. A bit touched in the head, an impractical man, but a genius. He read H.G. Wells' *The Time Machine* and became obsessed with time travel. He devoted his life to it. He concluded, after years of research, most done in this very room, that although mathematics may allow it, one cannot travel backwards in time. One can, however, take great leaps forward, so that what appears to the traveler as the blink of an eye is to the rest of humanity the passing of decades."

"So you're from the past?" I asked.

"We are all from the past, Captain, but yes, I was born in 1893," he said. "You know, I did not intend to kill you, just to persuade you."

"Persuade me?" I asked. "Of what? That you built a time machine?"

"I hear from your tone that you are skeptical. I suppose it is your job to be skeptical. But it is real. Herman used what he learned and built this device. If the world had known about his accomplishment, he would have won a Nobel Prize." While the man spoke, I walked over to inspect the box, my gun still trained on him.

"Herman," he continued, "calculated that the time required to accelerate and decelerate the traveler to the speed of light meant the minimum time forward would be twenty years. One could, in theory, send someone forward infinitely, but power demands and metal fatigue made anything over one hundred years impractical. He also predicted the deceleration process would incapacitate travelers on arrival, leaving them with weakened hearts and delirium for about one day. You have already seen proof of that."

"So, why did you 'travel' here?"

"As I told you, I am a physician. My formal medical career, however, came to an untimely end due to some unfortunate situations and misunderstandings. I am a brilliant surgeon, but I was reduced to exercising my talents at night in this basement, performing abortions and extracting bullets from gangsters. It was so far beneath me. But this work taught me that many people have problems they would like to disappear—that they will pay handsomely to make disappear. That machine," he gestured with his head, "makes problems disappear."

"What about Goldie?" I asked.

"Ah, Goldie. When I explained my revelation to Goldie, that Herman's machine would be our path to riches, she did not share my joy. She said I was horrible and spat at me. She told me she wanted nothing more to do with me. She threw me out of her home. As I walked away, hurt and surprised, someone tapped me on the shoulder. I turned to see Goldie's younger sister, Pearl, her face flush from running after me. Pearl had been listening to our conversation, and she thought her sister was foolish. I deserved, she said, someone who would help me. Pearl kissed me and confessed her love. I took Pearl home that night."

"Three months later, there came a knock on my door late one evening. Herman and I had reached a nadir in our fortunes and had been forced to dismiss the staff, so I was the one to answer. I found Goldie and Pearl standing there. Pearl was tearful, while Goldie's face contorted in rage. Pearl, Goldie said, had come to her crying, worried she was pregnant. Pearl hesitated at first to tell Goldie, but then she confessed that I must be the father."

"Well then," I said, "perhaps I should marry her."

"Goldie slapped me hard across the cheek. 'You vet keynmol do that!,' she growled, for she tended to lapse into a barbaric Yiddish when she was angry. 'You will repair this, and then you will leave Pea and me alone!'"

"I brought Pearl down here, laid her on the table where you were just sitting, and sent her off to sleep with some heroin —it is such a useful drug. As I performed the abortion, I realized how I could get back at them and started another procedure. I returned upstairs to let Goldie know the operation was a success and gave her a little heroin as a peace offering, for Goldie could never resist it. As she reclined in her chair drifting into oblivion, I told her how I had converted the operation to a hysterectomy to make sure Pearl would never have this problem again, no matter how many times I would enjoy her favors." He paused to smile.

"Goldie tried to rouse herself, to get angry with me, but the heroin would not let her. I told her not to worry, that we were going to solve her problem too. I then woke up my brother to let him know we had our first client. He didn't question who or why; he was too excited. We carried the box —for such a remarkable machine it is not very heavy—out of the lab and into our backyard."

"Why did you do that?"

"You are listening. Good. That is an excellent question. The machine lets people travel in time, not space. Herman figured it would be safer for people to arrive in the future above ground. There is a ventilation shaft in the corner behind you that reaches up to the lawn, and we used it to run wiring from this room. As Herman prepared the box, I went back in, stripped Goldie naked, and carried her outside to put her in the machine."

"Why naked?" I asked.

"Herman hypothesized different items might accelerate or decelerate at different rates, so anything extraneous could mutilate a traveler. Herman was so excited to use the machine, he didn't even realize who I put in. After a brief discussion, we opted to send her 90 years into the future. Well, Herman turned on the machine, which hummed to life, and flipped the switch. There was a bit of rattling for about ten seconds and then abrupt quiet. We feared at first it had not functioned or even might have broken, but when we opened the lid, Goldie had vanished!"

"Herman was ecstatic. He wanted to call the papers, but I convinced him that since we could never have immediate proof, he needed to keep the research secret for now. I would recruit more subjects, and he could work on fine-tuning the device and working out his calculations."

"I returned to Pearl, woke her, and told her the operation had been a success and that Goldie had left, but that I would like her to stay. I kissed her gently on the lips. Pearl consented with a big grin, no doubt imagining our future together. Pearl was pretty and useful to me in that way, and she did not suffer from Goldie's misgivings of conscience. Pearl was, however, a simple child who lacked Goldie's intelligence. I quickly realized I could not trust her discretion, and I grew tired of her silly affections, which only reminded me of her preferable sister. She also began asking to return home to collect her things and say goodbye. I, of course, could not allow that.

"Pearl did, however, help secure my first paying customer, a gentleman who sought to dispose of a mistress who threatened his marriage. The customer, a minor industrialist whose money derived from the exploitation of coal and those who extracted it, brought the woman to my home on the pretense of a dinner invitation. We sat drinking cocktails for an hour until the mistress, Lily was her name, passed out from the additive to her highball. I collected the fee from the gentleman and told him to leave, that his issue would be solved by morning.

"I carried the woman into a parlor to prepare her for her journey. As I undressed her, it occurred to me I might solve two problems at once. I injected her with a bit of heroin, as was now my protocol, and called Pearl over. I told her I had a bit extra and perhaps she might want to join me in a bit of an indulgence. She readily agreed.

"Herman, meanwhile, was setting up the box on the lawn. He thought we had willing time travelers paying for a unique experience. Again, he hadn't pressed me for details when I told him we had two new willing subjects rather than just one. He was a bit surprised when he saw Pearl was one of them, but I told her she had been begging me to see the future, that she wanted to be a part of his great scientific experiment, and that I wanted to indulge her, even if we weren't being paid. That was all the explanation Herman needed.

"So we put Pearl in first. I suggested we try, for experimentation sake, and to limit wear on the machine, a shorter time forward, say, sixty-six years, in honor of our address. Herman thought for a moment and then agreed. So Pearl was sent. We were about to send Lily as well when Herman stopped. He realized, he said, if we sent them one right after the other at around the same time, they might arrive with their bodies entwined in one another, likely killing them in a gruesome mess. I proposed adjusting the time to about one month later, which he thought sufficiently safe.

"It would not matter. Synthesizing what Herman explained to me about the machine with my medical training, I calculated that the way the wave function of the machine periodically coincided with that of human cardiac electrical activity, people sent at intervals of around eleven years would reach their futures without a heart beat. They might appear otherwise okay but would arrive dead. I believe I was right about that, no?" He paused to gauge my reaction.

"One week later, we had another customer. This one was delivered to us already medicated. Herman, who answered the door, wondered why two thugs were dropping off a drugged woman, and as I pocketed their money, I explained that she had been eager but very nervous. We again prepared the setup on the lawn. Herman wanted to try a different year, but I insisted we just move the time forward one month from its last setting—it would be a pattern we could remember—and this is what we did. Another success.

That night, Herman woke me from sleep, shoving my shoulder hard. I don't know how he had obtained it, but he was pointing a gun at me.

"'You knew!' he said. 'Sixty-six. You knew! You killed them.'

"'We,' I told him. 'You flipped the switch. I took your wonderful machine and found a practical use for it. We are now saved thanks to your genius and my intuition. What do you think is paying off our debts, reviving our fortunes? Do you want to continue to live here, to pursue your experiments?'"

"Herman inched closer. His left eye was twitching and his right arm shaking, which let the barrel of the pistol graze my forehead. 'Please,' I told him, 'put the gun away.' He shook his head. He then put the gun to his own temple and blew his brains all over my bedroom. I wish he hadn't done that. If only he had taken the time to understand…"

He sighed. "Herman was dead, and his death led me to my final solution. I needed to send Herman's body somewhere it would never be discovered. So I moved the machine to the corridor leading to this room, put my brother in it, and set the time for thirty years. He vanished."

"Although I had to continue without him, the enterprise thrived. I planned to send all my customers thirty-three years into the future, all from that same place in the corridor. No one ever discovered what I was doing. Flush with cash, I could indulge many other interests. Alas, these indulgences caught up with me and gave me the need to find my own escape. Rather than emigrate to another country, I would flee to the future as well, timing my arrival about six months before Goldie's. I blocked and hid the entrance to this room from the house. I then converted my assets to gold and secured them here. I let it be known I was considering traveling abroad and booked passage to Hamburg. I then sealed myself here. In resetting the dials for my own journey in time, I realized that, due to a small error, I had been sending people thirty years into the future rather than thirty-three, an error that meant they would all arrive alive. To remedy my mistake, I packed the corridor with dirt and placed wooden planks to prevent entrance into this room."

"You mean those people …"

"Yes, they awoke to find themselves buried alive, in most cases their bodies intertwined with the rotting corpses and skeletons of others. It probably wasn't a pleasant death. But as I was saying,..."

"You've given me more than enough to arrest you for multiple murders."

"By all means, Captain, arrest me. I am sure everyone will believe your tale of a time machine, of a killer from the past. They will not be suspicious in the least about your clandestine meeting with Mr. Jessup, who then winds up dead."

"Dead?"

"He is in the van now. Your fingerprints are on the bags holding his body. You are also captured on his camera system, and, although I am still learning about how computers work, I am fairly certain it photographed you and kept a record of your looking at Goldie's arrival. Maybe you are hiding something else? Captain, please understand, as far as the world knows, I am a mere hired laborer while you are the mastermind. The press still loves to print stories of corrupt police officers, no? Of the mighty falling? Of justice perverted?"

"So," he continued, "You have two choices. You can, as you propose, arrest me and hope to explain this all away before it destroys you. Or, you can help me move Jessup and all those bones from the truck back down here to the machine, dispose of them, take a share of the gold, and never worry about this again. Make it a problem for the future."

"I won't compromise myself ..."

"Captain, we all make compromises."

IX

I was announced as the new commissioner that Friday and sworn in the following week. When the mayor lost her election one year later, the incoming administration begged me to stay on, promising me complete control of the department's direction and whatever resources I might need. I had one request. Since my career had been made at Golden Park, I always had an affinity for the mansion there and would appreciate anything that could be appropriately done to help me acquire it now that it was back on the market. Mr. Douglas Jessups, the beneficial owner of the entity that purchased the house, had disappeared, and no one knew what had become of him. In his absence, the acting corporate officer thought it best to dispose of the home rather than pay for upkeep, and I bought it for quite a reduced price. When I took possession two months later, the corridor was still packed off and hidden, just as I had left it that Sunday. The place still needs some work, but it's livable.

The second evening in my new home, the doorbell rang around eight. It was Santiago, now newly minted Sgt. Santiago. She apologized for coming to see me at home and after work, but she had something she needed to ask. I invited her in, and we sat in the living room, in almost the same spot Jessup and I once met. She had never, she said, been able to stop thinking about the woman in the hospital. With her new authority as sergeant, she had looked into the closed case file and discovered I never submitted any samples to the lab for analysis. She wanted to know why.

"An oversight," I told her. "That was around the time I became commissioner, right? Some things just got lost in the transition."

"I see," she said.

"There hasn't been any more activity around here, has there? I mean, now that I'm a resident, I should know for my own safety."

"No," she said. "But, when I looked at the footage from the cameras..."

"The cameras?" I said. "The ones I told you to take down?"

"Yes," she continued. "I took them down and stored them in the file. However, I wasn't able to do that until that Monday morning, and I'd never looked at the footage until today. Commissioner, what were you doing here that Sunday?"

"Sergeant," I said, rising from my chair, "I have to commend your diligence. I see a lot of me in you, your refusal to give up on a case. It's why, like me, you're on the fast track to your future. The truth is, there was another investigation at the time, one which I was not at liberty to disclose then, but I think I can do so now. But first, can I get you a drink?"

"Well..." she said.

"C'mon. We're colleagues, and we should drink to your promotion. A word of advice—you're not going to go far turning down hospitality."

"Okay, well... sure. No, of course. Absolutely!" she replied.

I disappeared into the kitchen to pour two whiskeys. When the doctor threatened me in the basement, I'd called his bluff. I would "compromise," I said, if he showed me proof of the machine in action. I handed him one glass flask on the counter. "Send this," I said. He hesitated; he was not sure if it would work on something inorganic. I told him to do it, or I would haul him off to jail right then. So he put it in the box, turned the dials, and flicked the switch. There was a ten second hum and then nothing. He opened it, and... the flask was gone! I had him bring back down all the sacks, and each one similarly disappeared. As he finished with the last bag of bones, I whacked him over the head with a shovel, shoved him into the machine, and dispatched him as he deserved, ninety-nine years into the future. A corpse for some cop yet unborn to puzzle over. Justice served. Despite everything that had happened that Sunday morning, it was still fairly early, and if I left then, it would be unlikely that anyone would be the wiser. I couldn't take the machine with me, but I also couldn't quite bear to destroy it. Instead, I closed the "door" to the tunnel so it again looked like a wall and nothing else. I took Jessup's security computer, which I later destroyed, and left.

The first thing I did when I moved into the mansion was to check the corridor again. The time machine was still there. I would find a way to get it into the right hands. Until then, I would never use it.

But just now, I had a problem that probably wasn't going to go away. Sometimes, the best way to solve a problem is to put it off until tomorrow. Or many tomorrows.

"Sergeant," I said, returning to the room and handing her a glass, "Cheers. Now, this may sound a bit strange, but to answer your question, I think there's something in the basement you ought to see."

D.H. PARISH (he/him) is, like Dr. Jekyl, a physician by day who indulges a darker side at night, albeit only with the written word. He has had stories presented on multiple horror podcasts, including *Scare You To Sleep, Creepy, Nocturnal Transmissions,* and *The Morbid Forest* and appear in horror and speculative fiction print anthologies and magazines. He lives in Pennsylvania with his wife. You can find more information at his website, dhparishstories.com.